For my family

–Emily McDermott

For Scarlet & Zelda

–Hannah Adams

LITTLE ONE

Written by Emily McDermott
Illustrated by Hannah Adams

Before you were born, Little One WHEN YOU SWAM IN MY BELLY LIKE A FISH

Before I ever
knew your
hopes & dreams
YOUR HAPPINESS
WAS MY ONLY WISH

Before you
ever opened your
eyes, my son
BEFORE YOU GAZED AT
ME WITH WONDER & JOY

*I knew that
I would see
heaven reflected*
IN THE EYES OF MY
SWEET LITTLE BOY

Before I ever held you, Little One SMELLED YOUR SWEET SKIN, SOFT AND WARM

I knew that I'd want to hold you forever AND PROTECT YOU IN MY LOVING ARMS

Before I ever heard you laugh, my son HEARD YOUR GIGGLE OF PURE DELIGHT

I knew that I'd do anything to make you smile

AND MAKE YOU HAPPY EACH DAY & NIGHT

Now that you're here, I don't need to think

ABOUT ALL THAT I KNEW "BEFORE"

Because what matters now is that you're loved today

AND TOMORROW I'LL LOVE YOU EVEN MORE!

The End

Made in the USA
Lexington, KY
09 September 2017